FABIO
THE WORLD'S GREATEST
FLAMINGO DETECTIVE

THE CASE OF
THE MISSING HIPPO

LAURA JAMES
illustrated by EMILY FOX

BLOOMSBURY
CHILDREN'S BOOKS

NEW YORK LONDON OXFORD NEW DELHI SYDNEY

BLOOMSBURY CHILDREN'S BOOKS
Bloomsbury Publishing Inc., part of Bloomsbury Publishing Plc
1385 Broadway, New York, NY 10018

BLOOMSBURY, BLOOMSBURY CHILDREN'S BOOKS, and the Diana logo
are trademarks of Bloomsbury Publishing Plc

First published in Great Britain in March 2018 by Bloomsbury Publishing Plc
Published in the United States of America in August 2019
by Bloomsbury Children's Books

Bloomsbury books may be purchased for business or promotional use. For information on
bulk purchases please contact Macmillan Corporate and Premium Sales Department at
specialmarkets@macmillan.com

Library of Congress Cataloging-in-Publication Data
Names: James, Laura, author. | Fox, Emily (Emily A.), illustrator.
Title: Fabio the world's greatest flamingo detective : the case of the missing hippo /
by Laura James ; illustrated by Emily Fox.
Other titles: Case of the missing hippo
Description: New York : Bloomsbury, 2019.
Summary: Flamingo detective Fabio and his giraffe associate, Gilbert, investigate
when a singing hippopotamus disappears during auditions for a talent show
being staged to save the failing Hotel Royale.
Identifiers: LCCN 2018051684
ISBN 978-1-5476-0216-2 (paperback) • ISBN 978-1-5476-0217-9 (hardcover)
Subjects: | CYAC: Mystery and detective stories. | Flamingos—Fiction. |
Animals—Fiction. | Kidnapping—Fiction. | Talent shows—Fiction. |
Hotels, motels, etc.—Fiction.
Classification: LCC PZ7.1.J385 Fab 2019 | DDC [Fic]—dc23
LC record available at https://lccn.loc.gov/2018051684

Typeset by Janene Spencer
Printed in China by Leo Paper Products, Heshan, Guangdong
2 4 6 8 10 9 7 5 3 1 (paperback)
2 4 6 8 10 9 7 5 3 1 (hardcover)

All papers used by Bloomsbury Publishing Plc are natural, recyclable products
made from wood grown in well-managed forests. The manufacturing processes
conform to the environmental regulations of the country of origin.

To find out more about our authors and books visit www.bloomsbury.com and
sign up for our newsletters.

In a small town on the banks of Lake Laloozee lives the world's greatest flamingo detective. His name is **Fabio**. He's not tall or strong, but slight and pink. And he's very, very clever.

At his side for every case is his friend and associate, **Gilbert**, a giraffe terrible at the art of disguise but good at asking questions— sometimes even the right ones.

Chapter 1

As the sun began to set, Fabio and his great friend Gilbert walked through the splendid doors of the Hotel Royale. It was time for a cool glass of pink lemonade. Little did they know, as they were greeted by Smith, the hotel's owner, this pleasant place was about to be hit by a big mystery.

"Good evening, gentlemen."

Smith led them through the grand

but entirely empty lobby to the terrace at the back of the hotel, where they took their usual table by the pool.

At the bar a rhino rustled her newspaper.

Smith was a grumpy old vulture. Fabio had known him for many years. He ran the hotel with his sister, Penelope, who was a temperamental chef. Penelope's daughter, Violet, had just started working at the hotel too.

"It's very quiet in here this evening," commented Fabio, taking note of his surroundings.

"Yes," agreed Smith unhappily. "Business is slow. Violet has decided to hold a talent contest to liven the place up a bit." He presented Fabio and Gilbert with the lemonade menu and gave a small bow. "It won't work," he added gloomily. Smith, Fabio knew, did not welcome Violet's schemes. She was going to have a tough time changing things at the hotel.

Fabio spotted Violet putting up a poster advertising the contest.

Smith beckoned her over. "Violet, come and say hello to Mr. Fabio and his good friend Gordon."

"Gilbert," Gilbert corrected him. He'd been correcting Smith for years.

"Hello, Mr. Fabio, Mr. Gilbert," said Violet. "Lovely evening, isn't it?"

The rhino at the bar thrust her nose over the top of her newspaper. "I knew it!" she exclaimed. "You're that pink detective, aren't you?"

Fabio politely tipped his hat. "Fabio, the world's greatest flamingo detective, at your service, madam."

"The name's Daphne. But everyone calls me the General. I'm just back from safari. Shall I join you?"

Without waiting for a response, the General put her newspaper under her arm, bustled over to their table, and took a seat between Fabio and Gilbert. It was a bit of a squeeze.

No sooner had the General sat down than there was an enormous splash as a hippo launched herself off the diving board and into the pool, drenching everyone at the table.

"Golly!" exclaimed Gilbert. "What a splendid dive!"

"That's Julia," said Smith, attempting to dry Fabio off with the tablecloth. "She's a singer."

"I'm so sorry," said Julia, emerging from the water.

The General removed her reading glasses to take a close look at Julia while wringing out her second-best shawl in a huff.

"I didn't know anyone was sitting there," Julia continued. "Did I get you wet?"

"Only a little," said Gilbert untruthfully. "But it was worth it. You dive beautifully."

Fabio offered Julia a seat. "Please, join us. Perhaps, Smith, you could bring pink lemonade for everyone?"

Smith went off to fetch the drinks and the General charged after him urgently, still wringing out her shawl.

Julia grabbed a towel and sat down next to Fabio.

Gilbert moved his chair to make room for her while Fabio made the introductions.

"It's nice to see some new faces down by the pool," Julia said. "The band and I have been the only ones here all day." She pointed to three crocodiles who were trying to catch the last rays of sun on the far side of the pool.

Noticing they were being watched, they waved.

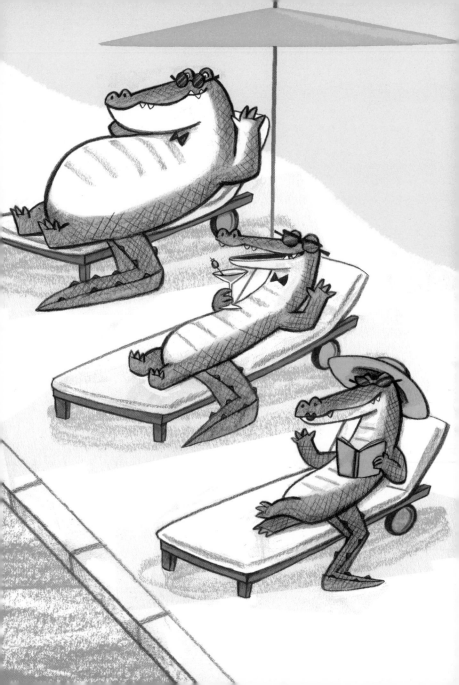

Gilbert returned an enthusiastic wave and Fabio tipped his hat to them.

Violet came back with a fresh tablecloth.

"I'm sure Violet's talent contest will help cheer the place up a bit," said Fabio, smiling at the young vulture.

"Oh, I do hope so," said Violet. "I've got lots of ideas. I just need this first one to really take off so that my uncle will let me do more."

"We're going to enter," said Julia. "We were discussing it this afternoon."

Just then Smith returned to the table with the drinks, and the General also reappeared, looking considerably drier.

"ACHOOOOOO!" The General sneezed dramatically. "Oh, dearie me.

I'm coming down with a cold. It must have been all that water."

Fabio narrowed his eyes, the way he did when he thought something out of the ordinary was happening. "You've come down with a cold very quickly," he commented.

"You can't be ill now," Violet said to the General. "You're the head judge for my talent contest."

"I'm sorry, Violet, but when I catch a cold, I really catch a cold," replied the General. "I certainly won't be able to judge the contest."

"But what shall I do?" moaned Violet. "The auditions are tomorrow!"

"Perhaps you should ask Fabio to be head judge," suggested Julia.

"No, no, no, my friend," protested Fabio, shaking his head.

"It's a lot of hard work . . . ," the General began, only to be interrupted by an enthusiastic Gilbert.

"You'd be a great judge!"

"Please will you do it?" urged Violet. "If we have someone as famous as you judging the competition, we're sure to bring in a crowd."

"That's settled then," said Julia, raising her glass and not giving Fabio a chance for further protest. "To the new head judge of the talent contest."

"To Fabio!" Gilbert chimed in.

The General picked up her handbag,

seemingly annoyed by the whole thing. "Fine," she said. And then, as if remembering something, "By the way, good luck with that slippery snake and no-good bird. You'll be sorry you agreed to this, mark my words."

And with that, she marched off.

"What do you think she meant by that?" asked Gilbert when the General was out of earshot.

"She was talking about the other two judges," said Violet. "George Percy the Third is a local used-car salesman. He's got a reputation for doing shady deals, but he used to be a child star, so I thought he'd make a good judge. Enid is the other judge. She's a secretary bird. She used to be a prima ballerina and now runs the Laloozee Ballet Academy. She's very ambitious for her students. George

Percy sold her a car a year ago that broke down as soon as she left the garage. They haven't gotten along since, but I didn't know that until after I'd asked them both to judge. There are rumors about Enid too. My cousin's friend's friend said she's been spending the ballet school money on fancy knitting needles."

"Embezzlement!" exclaimed Fabio.

Gilbert looked blank.

"Theft," Fabio whispered.

"Oh, right," said Gilbert.

"Nothing has ever been proven," said Violet, "but she's always on the lookout for extra funding for the academy. She and George Percy bicker all the time."

Fabio groaned. The idea of judging the talent contest was getting worse by the minute.

"Sounds like you're going to have your work cut out for you," said Gilbert, after Violet had left them and Julia had returned to the pool to do a couple of lengths before dinner.

Fabio took a careful sip of his pink lemonade. He was deep in thought. Finally, as if making a decision, he turned to his companion. "I'm going to need you to be my eyes and ears during the contest, Gilbert. There's something strange going on here."

"Is there?" asked Gilbert. "Say, shall I put on a disguise?"

"If you must," replied Fabio.

Chapter 2

The following morning, Fabio and Gilbert walked into the Hotel Royale's ballroom. The auditions for the talent contest were about to begin. There was a stage at one end of the room, and circular tables were laid out for the audience. Fabio stood at the door and took it all in. He would make sure the talent show was a success. The Hotel Royale closing would, in his mind, be an unthinkable tragedy.

Violet's advertising campaign had worked well. Dozens of hopeful contestants were filling the hotel. The food and drink orders were coming thick

and fast, and head chef Penelope was
furiously shouting at her kitchen staff,
who were totally unprepared for such a
large turnout.

Fabio set up a methodical system for the auditions, and each act was given a number. Once he was happy that things would run smoothly, he took his seat as head judge. Gilbert, disguised as a stagehand, hid in the wings at the side of the stage.

On Fabio's right was the dubious-looking boa constrictor, George Percy the Third. He'd clearly had a good breakfast.

On Fabio's left was the secretary bird, Enid, who was knitting her godson a new sweater. The snake and the secretary bird were already having a spat. Enid had accused George Percy of making her drop a stitch. Unintentionally or not, George Percy had then stuck his tongue out. Being a snake, he stuck his tongue out quite a lot, so it was hard to tell.

Enid was determined to take offense.

Fabio would not be drawn into the argument. "Shall we begin?" he asked, looking at the long line of noisy contestants ready to get onstage.

First in line was Violet. She'd brought some sheet music with her, which she handed to the accompanist—a baboon called Ernest.

"In the key of *H*," she whispered to him.

Ernest took the sheet music without saying a word. He'd seen it all before.

The room fell silent.

Violet stepped into the spotlight.

"Go ahead, Violet," said Fabio. "Whenever you're ready."

Violet nodded to Ernest, who began to play.

Fabio settled back into his seat and waited.

Violet attempted the first note: "*LaaaaaAAAAAAAaaaaAAAAAAAAAA AaaaaAAAAA.*"

As Fabio had suspected, vultures really can't sing. Everyone except for Fabio and Ernest had their fingers in their ears (Fabio because of his legendary good manners, and Ernest

because he was a true professional and continued to play the piano).

Smith, who was in the wings opposite Gilbert's hiding place, could be heard muttering something about Violet getting back to work.

Fabio signaled for Violet to stop.

"But I haven't hit the high notes yet!" she protested. "I'm *really* good at those!"

"That was lovely, Violet," he said. "You're through to the competition."

"Are you completely mad?" hissed George Percy the Third.

"Or deaf?" whispered Enid aggressively.

"She's the reason the contest is taking place," said Fabio quietly. "What harm can it do?"

"She'll empty the place," replied Enid.

"You're through," Fabio confirmed, ignoring his fellow judges' comments. A plan was beginning to form in his head. "We look forward to hearing you sing in the contest, Violet."

George Percy the Third and Enid looked at each other, for once in agreement.

Violet was ecstatic.

Smith harrumphed in the wings and

told her to go and look after the family of impala who had just checked in.

Next up, from the savannah, were a hyena and two jackals who had formed a calypso band. They were followed by an elephant father-and-son magic act. The son proved difficult to cut in half, but he made everyone laugh so they went through too.

Then Fabio noticed Enid stopping her knitting as a graceful cheetah took to the stage.

"My name is Carl, and I shall be telling the story of the three little pigs through the form of interpretive dance," he told the judges proudly.

"This will be marvelous, I'm sure," murmured Enid.

"Please begin," said Fabio.

It was a complicated piece, made all the more difficult by the fact that the cheetah had to play the parts of the wolf *and* pigs numbers one, two, and three.

George Percy the Third got a fit of the giggles, and an unamused Enid brandished a knitting needle at him. To prevent a full-blown fight, Fabio put the cheetah through to the

competition. A breathless Carl bowed his thanks and exited stage left.

After that came a troupe of cancan-dancing zebras, a chameleon comedian, and an aardvark who read poetry.

In all, the judges watched more than twenty acts and, somehow, they all made it through to the big night. Fabio was getting his way. He knew

that the more contestants there were, the more supporters there would be on the night. He was eager to back Violet's entrepreneurship, but he was also eager for his favorite pink lemonade spot to remain open for business.

"I don't know what happened!" sighed George Percy the Third as a baton-twirling mongoose headed off stage. "Is it time to go home yet?"

"Not quite," said Fabio. "Where's Julia?"

Enid shrugged.

"Who's Julia?" asked George Percy the Third.

"I'm Julia!" said the hippo, stepping into the spotlight.

Behind her was her band. She introduced them.

"Slapping that bass, we have Kevin." Kevin plucked the strings on his double bass.

"On sax, we have Delicious Delilah."
Delilah swung her saxophone around
and let rip some glorious notes.

"Aaaand," said Julia, "last but by no
means least, may we have an amazing
drum lick from Tiny Bob?" Tiny Bob
grinned as he bashed his way around
the drum kit, ending dramatically on the
cymbals.

The watching crowd was spellbound.

As the band started up, Julia moved
closer to the microphone and began to
sway her hips in time with the music.

Fabio tapped his foot and even

George Percy the Third and Enid caught the beat. This promised to be good.

But just as Julia opened her mouth to sing, the room was plunged into darkness.

The band stopped playing in a mish-mash of notes, and Gilbert almost gave himself away by exclaiming, "Oh golly!" very loudly.

"This is a fiasco," hissed George Percy the Third.

"Will someone turn the lights on?" Fabio commanded calmly through the chaos.

Eventually the lights came back on.

"Where's Julia?" asked Fabio.

The hippo was nowhere to be seen.

"She must have gone offstage," reasoned George Percy the Third.

"She's not here," said Gilbert, untangling himself from the curtain. "Is she with you, Smith?"

"What are you doing there, Gordon?" asked Smith, taken aback.

Gilbert looked crestfallen at being recognized.

"Smith, is Julia with you?" asked Fabio.

"She's definitely not here," replied Smith. "I think I'd notice a hippo, don't you?"

The band was distraught. They rushed all over the ballroom searching for their lead singer.

"Someone call the police," said Fabio. "Nobody is allowed in or out of this room until they arrive. Gilbert, guard the door."

"Don't you think you're going overboard, Fabio?" asked Smith, casting a mean glance at Gilbert. "She probably just got stage fright."

"That hippo was born to be on the stage," countered Fabio. "She would never get stage fright."

"I'll phone the police," said Violet.

The Laloozee police took their time arriving. They were not famous for their efficiency, since they were just a bunch of lazy warthogs led by the laziest of the lot: Chief Inspector Duff.

Duff finally shuffled his way into the ballroom.

"Here's our criminal," he said, trying to fit some handcuffs onto Gilbert. "He was hanging around outside the door, looking shifty. What's he supposed to have done?"

"That is my associate," fumed Fabio.

"Uncuff him now. He's done nothing wrong."

"He looks like a criminal to me," said Duff. "Look at those eyes."

Everyone tilted their heads upward to look at Gilbert's friendly brown eyes.

"What evidence have you got?" asked Fabio.

"Uh . . . none, actually. I don't even know the crime yet."

"Precisely," said Fabio.

Reluctantly Chief Inspector Duff removed the handcuffs from Gilbert.

"I came as soon as I heard," puffed

the General, appearing behind Duff and Gilbert. "What's happening?"

"There's been a kidnapping," replied Fabio.

"Has there?" Duff removed a pencil from behind his ear and took out his notebook. "Description of the victim?"

"She's big and gray," Violet chimed in helpfully.

"Well, here she is," said Duff, pointing toward the General. "Case solved."

"That's not the victim," said Fabio. "Would you mind, Chief Inspector, if I took over the investigation?"

"Be my guest," replied Duff, replacing his pencil behind his ear. "If you think you can do a better job."

"I know I can," replied Fabio. "It is all just a matter of logic."

Chapter 3

Fabio returned to the judges' table. This time, however, it was for the much more serious matter of determining not talent, but truth.

Interviewing the witnesses was made doubly difficult by the simple fact that the crime had happened in the dark. Just as he had suspected, the accounts were varied and confused. Fabio asked the questions while Gilbert took notes.

In the end, the list of potential suspects was thin.

Enid

Enid: Well, I'd just completed a sleeve. Sleeves are always my downfall, so I was feeling pretty pleased with myself. The hippo was on the stage and then it went dark, and that's all I can tell you.

Fabio: I understand your godson is the dancing cheetah called Carl, and that he is the star pupil at your ballet academy. Were you trying to increase his chances of success by getting Julia out of the competition?

Enid: Of course not! He's got natural talent, that boy. He'll go far with or without this two-bit competition.

Fabio: But a win for him would give

your ballet academy some much-needed publicity, would it not?

Enid: Maybe.

George Percy the Third

Fabio: Did I hear you trying to do a deal on a nearly-new car with the elephant in the magic act?

George Percy the Third: You may have. I do deals all the time.

Fabio: Did you tell him you'd "get rid of the competition" to increase their chances?

George Percy the Third: Who told you that?

Fabio: I can't reveal my sources.

George Percy the Third: It's that bird, Enid, you need to be questioning. I wouldn't trust her as far as I could throw her, and that's not very far, 'cause I've hurt my back.

Fabio: How do you think Enid could have kidnapped a hippo?

George Percy the Third: Ballerinas are much stronger than they look. Even retired ones.

Violet

Fabio: Did you kidnap Julia because you were worried she was better at singing than you are?

Violet: Of course not. I'm very confident in my abilities as a singer. She's no competition for me!

Fabio: You took a long time contacting the police. Time enough to hide Julia, perhaps?

Violet: It wasn't my fault. The police took a long time to answer their telephone!

The General

Fabio: What made you turn up at the hotel when you have a cold?

The General: I heard the siren on the police cars, so I thought I'd check out what was going on.

Fabio: Is your cold better?

The General: ACHOOOOO! No, no better. I really ought to be in bed.

Fabio: Why did Violet select you to be a judge of the contest, do you think?

The General: I like to follow the arts. I

used to go on the stage quite a lot when I was a youngster. You know, pantomime, that sort of thing.

Ernest

Fabio: Did you kidnap Julia?

Ernest: No, I didn't. Why would I kidnap the only contestant who showed any sense of musicality? It would be madness!

Fabio: Fair point.

Smith

Fabio: From your vantage point in the wings, did you see anything significant?

Smith: I couldn't see anything. The lights went out.

"We don't seem to be getting anywhere," said Gilbert, miserably packing away his notebook and disguise. "I couldn't get a word out of Julia's band. And as for that elephant, he couldn't remember anything. Shall we go for a lemonade?"

"Slow down, my friend. I haven't questioned you yet."

"But I didn't do it!" said Gilbert. "If you thought I'd done it why did you tell Duff to let me go?"

"I know you didn't do it," said Fabio.

"Well, that's a relief," said Gilbert.

"But you may have noticed something without realizing," Fabio explained.

"Oh, right," said Gilbert.

"Tell me what you saw."

"Well, Julia was on the stage with her band, about to sing. You, George Percy the Third, and Enid were at your little judging table. Violet was by Ernest the accompanist."

"Who else?"

"The magician and his son were backstage, packing up, and the other contestants had sat down to listen to Julia sing. And, of course, Smith was on the other side of the stage from me, in the wings."

"Anything else?" asked Fabio.

Gilbert thought hard. "Now that you mention it, there was something a bit odd. A shadow."

"A shadow?"

"Yes, on the other side of the ballroom, near the doors," said Gilbert. "I only saw it out of the corner of my eye, before the lights went out."

"Mmm," mused Fabio. "There is always the possibility that Julia wasn't kidnapped at all."

"What do you mean?" asked Gilbert. "She has gone missing, hasn't she?"

"Yes, but it could have been staged," replied Fabio. "With no offense to Julia, you'd have to be very strong to kidnap a hippo."

"It was quick too," said Gilbert.

"Yes," agreed Fabio, narrowing his eyes. "You'd have to be very strong or very clever."

Chapter 4

The following day happened to be the biggest day in the Laloozee athletics calendar: the Gold Cup. Famous athletes from across the land had gathered to compete in track and field. Gilbert was a big fan of the event, and in a moment of weakness Fabio had agreed to attend the meet with his friend.

Fabio was not a sports fan, but he was someone who always stuck to his word. He reasoned that he could use the time to think about the evidence so far in the case of Julia's disappearance. And, knowing as he did that his key suspects would themselves be attending the games, he did not count it as wasted time.

Gilbert's car screeched to a stop outside Fabio's office on Plume Street. Fabio dusted himself off and cautiously climbed in.

"Are you ready?" asked Gilbert cheerily. "There's a real buzz in town today. Everyone's hoping the record is

going to be broken for the 100-yard dash."

Fabio was about to respond when Gilbert put his foot on the accelerator and they sped off. By the time they reached the track, Fabio had turned a nice shade of green.

"Here we are!" said Gilbert. "I've got us trackside seats—I'll show you."

"Oh good," replied Fabio unconvincingly.

The stadium was already full, and Gilbert explained all the different events to Fabio. The long jump was taking place not far from where they were sitting. Two athletes were competing for the gold medal—a gazelle who had excellent technique, and a young lioness who, although awkward in the air, was doing surprisingly well.

"The gazelle will win, of course," said

Gilbert knowledgeably. "She already has two gold medals to her name."

"I disagree," replied Fabio.

Sure enough, when the competitors attempted their final two jumps, the gazelle had a foul and the lioness jumped a personal best to take gold.

"How did you know that was going to happen?" asked Gilbert.

"It was just a matter of observation," replied Fabio. "The gazelle had a very slight limp and kept looking across at her coach, while the lioness seemed to be more self-assured. I knew it was her day."

It wasn't only the long jump where Fabio was one step ahead of the crowd. He correctly predicted the winners of the shot put and pole vault and the winning tug-of-war team.

Gilbert was amazed. "You seem to know everything before it happens," he said. "Still, the winner of the 100-yard dash is assured.

No prizes for guessing that one. See that ostrich over there?" Fabio followed his friend's gaze as the athletes taking part in the final and most celebrated race of the day came onto the track. "He's called . . ."

"Jay Jay Swift."

"How did you know that?" asked Gilbert.

"It's here in the program," confessed Fabio with a laugh. "Did you also know that both George Percy the Third's garage and Enid's Ballet Academy are sponsors of the race?"

"I didn't," replied Gilbert, looking over Fabio's shoulder at the program.

"The prize money is huge too," Fabio added, reading on.

Seven athletes were taking their places on the track when the commentator announced a surprise last-minute entry: "In lane eight, we have Hugo 'the Tank' Atkins."

There was an audible intake of breath from the crowd as a rather unfit-looking rhino took his place in lane number eight.

"How strange," said Gilbert. "I've never heard of him. He doesn't look

like a sprinter. Still, it won't affect the outcome. Everyone's here to see Swift beat his own record."

Fabio studied the athletes carefully as they were introduced. His eyes narrowed. Though they were waving to the crowd or doing their stretches in preparation for the race, they all seemed unnaturally

subdued. One athlete, a panther in lane two, even yawned.

They crouched down at the starter's orders, and on the gun the race began.

First out of the blocks was the Tank. He was huffing and puffing and taking the smallest of steps, but somehow he took the lead.

The panther from lane two was being helped along by a leopard in lane three. A wildebeest in lane six was lying down, snoring. Jay Jay Swift was trying to catch up with the Tank, but he was getting nowhere.

"They're all half asleep!" said Fabio.

It was true. The only competitor even approaching the finish line was the Tank. After a painfully long time and a lot of puffing and perspiring, Hugo "the Tank" Atkins won the 100-yard dash in the slowest recorded time ever: one minute, thirty-seven seconds.

The onlookers were so confused they forgot to cheer.

Once the other athletes had been helped over the line, the announcer's voice came over the loudspeaker.

"Ladies and gentlemen, please make your way to the presentation podium, where Hugo 'the Tank' Atkins will receive his gold medal!"

Fabio and Gilbert arrived just in time to see the General barge her way through the crowd and into the prize-giving area.

"Curious!" exclaimed Gilbert. "What

does the General have to do with the Tank?"

"I don't know," answered Fabio. "But doesn't she look well? Her cold seems to have cleared up nicely."

"This is an outrage," hissed George Percy the Third, slithering his way through the throng toward Fabio. "I'm going to request a closer look at the results."

"This race has been rigged!" It was Enid, hot on his tail. For the second time in two days they were in agreement. "The Tank has never won a race in his life. It was only because the other athletes were half asleep that he took first place."

"The General's only been training him for a week," added George Percy. "And now she's going to take half his prize money. Where has she been hiding him, anyway? He didn't pay to stay at the Athletes' Village like the other competitors."

"This sounds very suspicious," said Fabio, tipping his hat to Enid and George Percy the Third. "Gilbert, we've got work to do."

Chapter 5

"**B**ut shouldn't we be looking for Julia?" asked Gilbert as they walked through the Athletes' Village.

"Certainly," said Fabio.

"Oh," replied Gilbert, confused. "I thought we were trying to find out why the Tank won the 100-yard dash."

"We are doing both," replied Fabio.

The accommodation for the athletes was top of the line, but Fabio and

Gilbert were not going to get into the VIP residence reserved for the sprinters without a little help. Fabio had arranged for George Percy the Third and Enid to meet them at the entrance. Being

sponsors, they had access to this exclusive part of the village.

"You're going to solve this mystery, aren't you, Fabio?" asked Enid. "Sponsoring a rigged race reflects badly on my ballet academy."

"And on my garage," added George Percy.

"That's already got a bad reputation," sniped Enid.

George Percy definitely stuck his tongue out at her this time.

Once Fabio and Gilbert were safely

inside, George Percy and Enid left them to it.

There were bedrooms off a long corridor, and at the far end was a room marked Presidential Suite. All the rooms

had Do Not Disturb signs, and Fabio and Gilbert could hear the occupants snoring away.

"Let's see who's in the Presidential Suite," suggested Fabio.

Gilbert knocked on the door for him. There was no response.

He knocked again and then tried the door. It was locked.

"We're going to have to break the door down," said Fabio.

Gilbert picked up a nearby potted plant and was about to launch himself at the door when he was interrupted.

"What brings you here, gentlemen?" It was the General.

"We wanted to see the athletes' accommodations," lied Fabio. "We're thinking of becoming sponsors."

"We are?" beamed Gilbert, nonchalantly putting the plant down.

Fabio kicked his ankle.

"We are," Gilbert agreed.

"That's very interesting," said the General. "You

couldn't ask for better, and now that dear Tankie has won a medal, he can afford to stay here too. But I must ask

you to leave. This area is for authorized personnel only."

The General turned and strode purposefully down the corridor, fully expecting Fabio and Gilbert to follow her.

"I've spilled some soil on the carpet," said Gilbert anxiously. "I'd better clean it up."

"Leave it, Gilbert. You've given me an idea."

As they followed the General back down the corridor, Fabio spotted a plate outside one of the rooms.

"Pick that up," he whispered to Gilbert.

"Oh, cake!" said Gilbert. "My favorite."

"Don't eat it!" Fabio grabbed the cake from Gilbert, noticing as he did so the distinctive gold emblem of the Hotel Royale on the china. "That's evidence."

Chapter 6

Fabio and Gilbert returned to the ballroom at the Hotel Royale. Fabio wanted to test a theory he'd come up with on the way back from the Gold Cup, and he needed Gilbert's help.

"Why are we here?" asked Gilbert suspiciously. "Are you hoping to find more clues about Julia's disappearance? Do you know where she is yet?"

"You are full of questions," said Fabio,

leading Gilbert onto the stage. "Stand there for me and pretend you're Julia."

Gilbert stood where he was told, wriggled his bottom, and pouted his lips a little.

"It's okay," said Fabio, from the wings, "I meant just stand there. That's it, take one step forward . . ."

"Aaaaargh!" Gilbert yelled as he fell through a trapdoor on the stage.

"Sorry!" said Fabio. "Wrong lever."

Gilbert's head was now poking out of a hole in the floor.

Fabio pulled the lever next to it and

raised Gilbert back to the level of the stage.

"There are levers in the wings that operate a false floor," Fabio explained. "You often have them in theaters, so characters can disappear dramatically."

"So that's how Julia was kidnapped. She fell through the floor!"

"Precisely. But we're not going to

tell anyone about this yet. We still have to find Julia, and whoever did it might move her if they think we're onto them."

"Right," said Gilbert.

"Now I need to make a phone call to Chief Inspector Duff."

As night fell, Chief Inspector Duff and his team, on Fabio's instructions, staked out the VIP area of the Athlete's Village.

Out of the darkness came an unusual noise.

SQUEAK

SQUEAK

SQUEAK

It was accompanied by a light and was heading toward them.

"Stop right there!" ordered Chief Inspector Duff.

The squeaking stopped and the light fell to the ground.

"Well, what are you waiting for?" shouted Duff to his fellow warthogs.

"Chief," said the newest recruit, "we can't see! We forgot our flashlights."

"You idiots," said Duff. "You've let them get away!"

He approached the dropped flashlight. There on the floor, in the soil Gilbert had spilled, was a footprint. And next to it was a dining cart full of delicious food—all on Hotel Royale china.

And the footprint in the soil belonged to a bird.

Chapter 7

The following morning, Gilbert came to collect Fabio from his Plume Street office. Fabio was on the phone.

"So, you've found her?" asked Fabio. "Good . . . And she's safe and well? Good . . . What's that? You've made an arrest? You've done what . . . ? I'm coming down to the police station. In the meantime, ask everyone to gather

at the hotel. I'll explain everything when
we get there."

"What's happening?" asked Gilbert.

"They've arrested Penelope."

"But what I don't understand," said Gilbert, as he drove them through Laloozee toward the Hotel Royale, "is why anyone would want to kidnap Julia."

"I will explain all when we get to the hotel," said Fabio.

Duff had arranged for Fabio's suspects to gather on the stage: the General, Smith, Enid, George Percy the Third, and Violet.

"Fabio, you've got to help us—my mother is innocent," pleaded Violet, as the world's greatest flamingo detective entered the room.

"Do not fear," replied Fabio. "I intend to prove her innocence."

"Will this take long?" asked the General. "I want to go and see how the Tank is getting on."

"Cheat," hissed George Percy the Third.

"Snake," added Enid, then, looking at George Percy, "sorry, no offense."

"I have customers to attend to," grumbled Smith.

"But you don't," said Fabio. "This is how it all started, isn't it? With you not having enough customers at the Hotel Royale. You were worried about the business and you didn't believe in Violet's ideas, so instead you leaped at the chance to make some money in the most cowardly way possible."

"Oh really, Fabio, and how would I do that?"

"By kidnapping an heiress and holding her for ransom, of course."

There was a stunned silence. Smith turned red in the face.

"But, Fabio, we've been looking for Julia. There *isn't* an heiress," said Gilbert, getting frustrated.

"Isn't there?" asked Fabio. "Ask the General. She knows all about it."

All eyes turned to the rhino.

"I know no such thing," replied the General.

"Yes, you do," said Fabio. "The headline of the newspaper you were reading the other day said **MISSING HEIRESS**."

"How on earth did you notice that?" asked the General huffily.

"I notice a lot of things," said Fabio. "That's why I'm the world's greatest flamingo detective. Now, I don't normally read such sensational papers myself, but there was also a photograph of the missing heiress, wasn't there? And when Julia came out of the pool, you took off your glasses to look at her. It was then that you noticed who she really was. Julia is none other than Juliana de Glitzberger, the famous diamond heiress."

Violet gasped.

"And it was then," Fabio continued, "that you decided you'd kidnap her and

demand payment for her return. You'd had to come back from safari because you'd run out of money.

"Your original plan to raise some cash was to train the Tank for the 100-yard dash. But you'd been misled over his chances, and that money-making scheme looked decidedly doubtful.

"When you saw Julia dive into the hotel pool, a new plan began to form. You knew about the trapdoor on the stage from when you used to perform here in your youth. But to succeed, you needed two people. You never had a cold. You just used that as an excuse not to judge the contest and to put yourself in a good place to kidnap Julia. What you didn't anticipate was that I would become head judge and figure out your little scheme."

"Very clever, Fabio. But you've forgotten something. There's no way I could have done it. I arrived after the police."

"You appeared to arrive after the police, you mean," said Fabio. "You were at the other end of the ballroom. Right next to the light switch.

"All you needed was an accomplice
in the wings, so you turned to Smith."

"That's a lie!" said Smith. "I had nothing to do with that hippo's disappearance."

"You were the only one who could have pulled the lever," replied Fabio. "Gilbert was on the other side of the stage and he says the only person near the levers was you. It's got your feathers all over it."

"But where did they keep her?" asked Enid. "It's pretty difficult to hide a hippo."

"Smith had a delivery truck parked underneath the stage. Julia was lowered straight into it and enclosed in a big crate. It all happened in the dark, so she

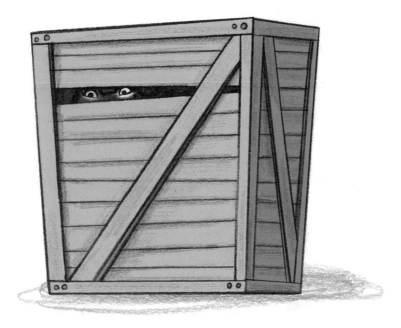

had no chance to figure out what was going on. Smith left a cake in there laced with sleeping powder. Once I'd finished questioning everyone, he was free to drive her to the Athletes' Village. They were used to him arriving in his truck, since the hotel is the official caterer. Under the cover of darkness, he led Julia to the Presidential Suite."

"At the village? That's disgraceful!" lisped George Percy the Third. "Does this have something to do with why the sprinters were so out of shape?"

"Exactly so," said Fabio. "Smith and the General wanted to keep Julia quiet until they'd successfully gotten their ransom money. Smith fed her a constant diet of her favorite chocolate cake laced with more sleeping powder. But Julia was beginning to feel homesick, so most of

the cake was left outside the Presidential Suite. The sprinters presumed it was for them and helped themselves.

"The Tank was the only one not affected, because he wasn't staying at the Athletes' Village. Not eating the sleeping-powder-laced cake meant he was able to win the race."

"But Duff arrested

Penelope because she's the chef," said Gilbert.

"Precisely. They added two and two and got five. They didn't realize that it was Smith who was delivering the food to Julia. They saw the bird footprint in the soil and knew that Penelope was the hotel chef, so made an incorrect assumption."

"You may release the prisoner," Duff ordered one of his detectives. A moment later, Penelope was free.

"Mother!" cried Violet, giving her a hug.

"But why did Julia go missing in the first place?" asked Gilbert.

"Because I want to sing," said Julia.

There was a collective gasp as Julia walked onto the stage. With her were Kevin, Delilah, and Tiny Bob. "I don't want the life of an heiress," she said. "I want to be a singer."

"But isn't your family worried?" asked Violet.

"They were, especially when they got the ransom note," said Julia. "But I've spoken to them now. I didn't mean to be missing for so long. I just needed to clear my head and spend some time with the band."

"So what's going to happen to my uncle and the General?" Violet asked Fabio.

"Duff?"

"Oh, right," said Duff, as if suddenly remembering what his job was. "I'm arresting you for kidnapping and—"

"You'll do no such thing!" said the General, and she began to run toward the door.

Quick as lightning Fabio nodded to Gilbert, who pulled the lever, and the General fell through the stage. She was

a bit bigger than Julia and, just as Fabio had planned, she got stuck.

Two of Duff's men cornered Smith and put handcuffs on him.

"As I was saying," said Duff. "I'm arresting you for kidnapping and mischievous villainy. You have the right to remain silent. Anything you say can and will be used against you. That goes for you too, Smith."

Duff's men hauled the General out of the hole in the stage and escorted her and Smith out of the Hotel Royale.

Everyone sighed with relief.

"What do we do now?" asked Julia.

"We carry on with the talent contest," said Violet. "There are people lining up outside, and tickets are sold out."

"That sounds like an excellent idea," said Fabio.

Chapter 8

The atmosphere in the ballroom was electric. The Hotel Royale hadn't been this busy since it first opened years ago.

"This is a great credit to you, Violet," said Fabio. "I think you can really turn this place around."

"Thank you," replied Violet, who had a newfound self-confidence. "Now that my uncle is out of the way, Mother and I

can run the hotel as we like. I think it will make her a lot less grumpy, not having him around. I'm not entering the contest tonight, if that's all right with you. I've got far too much to do, dealing with the customers. Besides, I thought I'd give Julia a chance!"

Fabio bowed.

"Oh and Fabio, I forgot to tell you . . ."

"Yes, Violet?"

"That story about Enid embezzling— is that how you say it?"

"That's right."

"It isn't true. My cousin's friend's friend said it was a different dance school, farther upriver."

"It's all right, Violet, I know," said Fabio. "I did a little detective work."

"Of course you did!" Violet smiled with relief.

Fabio took his seat at the judging

table. George Percy the Third and Enid were getting on well, for a change. It seemed their grievances over the 100-yard dash had united them. George Percy had agreed to give Enid a new car from his garage, and Enid was knitting George Percy a new beret.

Gilbert took his seat at the front table next to Julia's parents, only to be asked, politely, to move as no one behind him could see the stage. He went to stand in the wings instead.

After the house lights went down, the audience became quiet.

The evening passed by in a flash, and Violet thought she'd never served so many pink lemonades in her life. But it was the final act that everyone was waiting for.

Julia's band started to play. They got a beat going, and the mood in the ballroom changed. Then Julia stepped into the spotlight. She swayed her hips and tapped out the beat with her foot. Then she began to sing.

Fabio had never heard anyone sing like it.

By the end of the song the audience was on its feet, singing and dancing along

with her. There was simply no doubt who the winner was.

The other contestants and the judges joined Julia onstage as she and her band received the first Hotel Royale Talent Contest trophy.

"Isn't she amazing?" Violet shouted to Fabio above the noise of the crowd. "She's going to be our house singer," she added proudly.

"The Hotel Royale can go back to being the hottest venue in town," cheered Gilbert, busily dancing the funky chicken.

"And I can go back to being the world's greatest flamingo detective," laughed Fabio.

AVAILABLE NOW

LAURA JAMES is the author of the Adventures of Pug series, including *Captain Pug*, *Cowboy Pug*, and *Safari Pug*. Her love of storytelling began at an early age and led her to study writing for young people at Bath Spa University in England. She continues to live near Bath with her two dachshunds, Brian and Florence.

laurajamesauthor.com

EMILY FOX graduated from Falmouth University with a degree in illustration. She loves to experiment with color, funny stories, and animals, which means that Fabio is the perfect project for her. She lives in Bristol, England.

www.emilyafox.co.uk